Sins of the Father

Book Two
Pigeon Hollow Mysteries

Samantha Jillian Bayarr

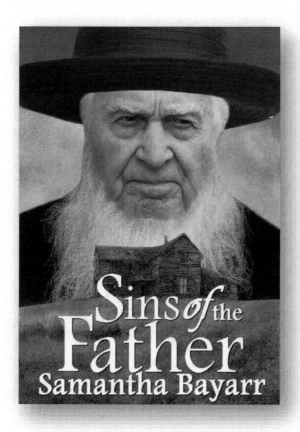

Sins *of* the
Father
Samantha Bayarr

ATTENTION READER: If you have not read the first book in this series, this book will not make sense to you, as it is a continuation in the series. Please take the time to read Book One: The Amish Girl, for the best reading experience.

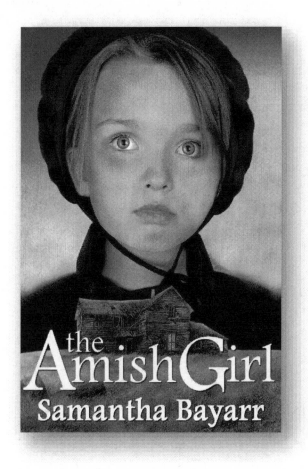

Ezekiel 18:19-20 New International Version (NIV)
19 "Yet you ask, 'Why does the son not share the guilt of his father?' Since the son has done what is just and right and has been careful to keep all my decrees, he will surely live. 20 The one who sins is the one who will die. The child will not share the guilt of the father, nor will the father share the guilt of the child. The righteousness of the righteous will be credited to them, and the wickedness of the wicked will be charged against them.

Chapter 1

Selma rose to her bone-chilled feet once more, her legs wobbly and weak, her energy nearly spent. She shivered, her stocking-clad feet and the hem of her long nightgown damp from the dirt floor of the cellar.

"Where did I leave my shoes?" she asked herself.

Did she even remember having shoes?

Her feet ached and throbbed, her toes numb from the cold floor, feeling as though she was standing barefoot on the frozen pond. Her teeth chattered as she wrapped the light quilt around her shoulders, working her way back up the ladder. Once again, when she reached the top wrung, her head pressed against the trapdoor. Bracing her shoulder against the thick wood, she pushed, putting her weight into it, but it was no use.

She was still trapped, still cold, and still alone.

"How many times do I have to do this, Lord, before you'll set me free?"

All traces of emotion had left her voice; she hadn't the energy for it. There had been a time when she'd been full of life, and her faith had been strong. Now, her faith had been shaken and tested, twisted and fallen to absence. There were days when she hadn't even felt human, much less, a child of God. Deep down she knew, but there had been no light at the end of this tunnel; no hope to hold onto, and no faith to carry her.

The stench from her makeshift chamber-pot in the corner was almost unbearable. It hadn't been emptied in the three days she'd been left alone. For the past two, it had nauseated her so much she had not been able to keep anything down. The linen cloth she kept over it was not enough to mask the odor.

Rats had rummaged through what little food she had left, and had eaten what she hadn't, which made her even more nauseated. She could hear them scavenging in the dark as she sat in the opposite corner.

"I'd rather die here, Lord, than for you to send him even one more time to release me!" she cried out into the dark. "Deliver me from this prison, Lord."

She curled up on the thin mattress in the farthest corner of the room, closing her eyes against the thoughts that plagued her. She'd lost all track of time, her health failing, and her spirit fading even faster. She laid there trying desperately to quiet the voices that crowded her mind. Anger and fear consumed her, but it no longer drove her to crave survival the way it once had. Giving up was easier. Each time she fought him, the punishment was greater, and the solitude grew longer.

The days in captivity had worn thin on her nerves and played tricks on her mind. Her son would likely no longer remember her, and she doubted she would recognize him. Surely he was a grown man by now, and had most likely given up hope of ever seeing her alive. Seeing his face again was the only thing that drove her anymore. She no longer cared anything about her own well-being; her only worry was for her child.

Unsure if she possessed the energy to fight, Selma laid in wait for that moment of weakness that would surely come. Her only bit of hope had come from the Mason jar she'd broken. It was the last canned peaches in the cellar, but it had spurred an idea. She prayed it was sharp enough to defend. It was her last resort, and if it failed to free her, she would use it to drain her own blood, having lost her will to live. She would take the desperate measure if need-be, just to put an end to her torture and imprisonment once and for all.

He'd taken everything from her, but she would not let him take away her right to finally have peace.

Zebedee lifted the latch to the cellar in the barn at the edge of his property. With a shotgun in his hand, he felt he was better-prepared this time. He would not let the out-of-control woman ambush him again. Surely she would recognize the threat that the gun posed, and would not make another attempt at escaping. He had become just desperate enough to teach her a lesson the hard way, if necessary. He hated that things had to be this way, but she just couldn't be reasoned with anymore. He'd tried to make things easy on her, he'd even tried to be good to her, but she'd made it clear she would have no part of him.

Truth was, she belonged to him, and he would be sure she understood that no matter what the cost.

Lowering himself into the cellar, Zeb was pleased to see she was sleeping soundly. He went to her, crouching down on his haunches, and smoothed the back of his hand across her ashen cheek. She had aged considerably, and her face was not as plump and beautiful as it once was when she was young, but he still loved her.

"I love you my dear, Selma," he whispered. "Why do you fight me so?"

In a fit of rage, Selma rolled over, drawing the thick piece of glass across his wrist, piercing his flesh.

"You don't love me!" she said through gritted teeth. "You only want to own me."

Selma scrambled to her feet, the element of surprise at catching Zeb off-guard long enough to drop the gun and grab his painful, bleeding wrist.

Selma scooped up the shotgun and held it at his back, contemplating what she'd only dreamt about for too many days. Her conscience, however, would not permit her to kill him, and so with one swift motion, she used the butt of the gun to hit him on the back of the head, knocking him out. His head hit the cellar floor with a thud, and she dropped the gun, scrambling her way up the ladder and out of the cellar into the cold, snowy night.

Chapter 2

Kyle stood on the bank of the large pond in pigeon Hollow and skipped a stone across the glassy shallow plane of water, counting five skips. It was his highest count during the time since he'd arrived at the large pond with his mother. She'd left him at the water's edge, making him promise he'd stay there while she approached a strangely-dressed man who was busy fishing, and ignoring her from what Kyle could see.

He watched the sinking sun flickering amber glitter across the light ripples of water as the wind swept across the surface. An occasional firefly dipped down, alighting the layer of edible particles, creating perfect circles that expanded, interrupting the glittery pattern. He tossed in a handful of autumn leaves just to watch them float out of sight, ferrying some of the bio-life to the other side.

"Don't do that, boy," the man's angry voice hollered to him. "You'll scare away the fish."

Kyle watched the motionless bobber a few feet offshore for movement, but didn't see any. The man wasn't doing it right. That wasn't the way his dad had taught him to fish, but he hadn't seen his dad since he was too young to remember. He'd forgotten almost everything about the man—except how to fish—and this man was not doing it right.

"Sorry," Kyle mumbled, kicking a light spray of sand into the water. "But you're not doing it right. My dad taught me how, and you won't catch any fish that way!"

The angry figure approached him, towering over him, the sun to his back. It cast a shadow over the faceless man, but Kyle could still see the disdain there regardless.

"You'll address me properly, boy," he said as he grabbed the scruff of his shirt pushing him to the ground.

His mother came to his rescue, touching the man's arms. "Please don't be so harsh," she begged. "He doesn't know you."

"He needs to learn proper manners and how to be respectful of his elders," the man's gruff voice sounded. "You don't teach him anything."

"He's only seven years old, and I'm doing the best I can on my own," she said, defending herself. "The boy needs a father."

"I told you not to bring him here. I don't want him here."

The man's thunderous voice rattled Kyle's ears, causing him to flinch. He looked into the stern pair of dark eyes that were deep-set, and fixed between a permanently cinched brow, which showed his disapproval with the young boy.

Kyle sucked in his breath and held it there, knowing something bad was about to happen.

Kyle bolted upright, scrambling from beneath the heavy quilts that wound around his legs so tight they were suffocating them. His breath heaved and gasped as he focused on the small bedroom in which he'd been staying in Caleb's *dawdi haus.*

His thoughts righting themselves, he still felt a little disoriented. Kyle struggled to remember the dream that had rattled him awake, leaving him with a grave feeling he knew the old man who'd conversed with his mother at the pond—almost as if the event really happened.

Before he could gain his bearings, a loud boom and a flash of light caught his attention, startling him further. He peered out the window beside the bed watching what looked like sparks flying off in the distance. They popped and cracked, shooting sparks like fireworks across the night sky.

If he didn't know better, he'd swear it looked like a transformer had blown, but he knew there was no such thing on the Amish property. He pressed his nose to the glass, watching the sparks light up the night sky, and realized they were coming from near the Yoder's barn at the edge of the property.

He pulled on his trousers right over the top of his long-johns, shivering as his bare feet touched the cold wood floor. He knew the noise was not thunder and the sparks would not be lightning, because such things did not happen in the winter.

Stuffing his feet into his boots, he looked around the dark room for a sweatshirt. When he located a heavy enough one, he pulled it down over his head and grabbed his heavy Carhartt jacket. It was bitterly cold when he'd gone to bed, and he could only imagine how much colder it was now. Last he'd heard on his truck radio just before dark, it was only 17°. He imagined the wind chill was likely 10 below.

As cold as it was, he wasn't up for investigating the loud boom or the sparks flying, but he feared something out there might catch fire if he didn't. Plus, he knew he'd never be able to sleep unless he checked it out, not wanting Caleb to have anything to worry about. He wanted his friend and his new wife to have a good honeymoon in

Florida. They weren't due back for another few days, and there would be no sense in worrying him needlessly.

Kyle shoved his hands into his leather gloves and shouldered out into the cold night air, the wind assaulting him with pelts of icy snow that stung his cheeks.

Knowing he could not get back toward the Yoder's barn without going through the cornfield that separated the barn from Caleb's new house, he contemplated going on foot, but when he heard a scream, he hopped in his truck and drove over the uneven, frozen soil toward the commotion, his truck dipping and bouncing over the tilled rows.

His headlights bounced off the barn and onto the ground, then, back up again as the truck rolled over the humps of tilled earth.

Was that a body in the snow?

Kyle pressed on the gas pedal, trying to push the truck faster over the dips and humps of frozen ground. He let off the gas when the front of the truck dipped hard, bringing the front fender down onto solid ground.

Stopping the truck short of the barn, he pulled around and aimed his headlights toward a figure lying motionless in the snow, sparks flying near the body.

Hopping out of the truck, Kyle left the door open and ran toward the figure he now realized was a woman. She lay there, face pushed into the snow, a blue, flannel nightgown clinging to her wet figure, brownish gray hair falling out from where it was loosely pinned at the nape of her neck.

He rolled her over, pulling off his heavy jacket to wrap her in. "Can you hear me?" he asked the older woman.

She groaned and looked up at him, her lashes fluttering open and closed. "Help me," she said weakly.

He tucked his arms under her frail frame to lift her out of the snow when she clenched his arm and looked him into the eye, a warm mist in her eyes.

"My baby!" she cried. "You came to rescue me."

"I'm here," he said to her, confusion clouding his judgment.

She'd obviously confused him with someone else.

Then her expression turned serious. "If you know what's good for you, son, you'll leave this place before it's too late!" she mumbled, then, she went limp in his arms.

Her warning sent shivers through his already cold body, as he lifted her up and cradled her against his sturdy frame. It was the sort of warning that was usually accompanied by an abundance of reasons behind it.

His gaze traveled to the area that shone brightly in the light from the headlamps of his truck that he'd left running. The transformer was attached to electric fence that surrounded the Yoder's barn, and he thought it odd. He'd thought it was strange when Amelia had run into barbed wire the night she'd run from him, and now Old-Man-Yoder had installed electric fence in its stead around his barn, with a voltage high enough to kill a herd of cows?

Why?

He looked at the woman in his arms, and noted the snow shovel she'd apparently used to break the voltage.

Was she breaking into the barn or *out* of it?

His mind filled with a million questions as he rushed her to the front seat of his truck and took the time to buckle her in for the bumpy ride back to the main road.

Whoever she was, she was in need of medical help, and he would not be able to give an explanation of her identity or her reason for being in the snow way out there without a coat or shoes.

Kyle hadn't planned on leaving the house on such a cold night, but now, it seemed, he'd be taking the strange woman to the hospital.

Chapter 3

Kyle rushed into the emergency room, the still unconscious woman in his arms.

"I need help!" he hollered.

A nurse rushed to his side with a wheelchair and helped Kyle lower the woman into it.

"What happened?" she asked.

"I have no idea," he said, out of breath. "I found her in the snow near a blown transformer. I'm house-sitting for a friend, and she was at the far edge of his property."

"Who is she?" the nurse asked.

"I have no idea," Kyle said. "I think she was trying to get into the barn back there, but it has electrical fence around it. I think she's homeless."

"We got a *Jane Doe*," the nurse hollered. "She looks like she's suffered malnutrition and hypothermia. I'm gonna need a room and a team right away."

Two nurses jumped up from behind the large desk that looked to be the hub of the emergency room. They each grabbed supplies and a cart, then, followed her down the hall.

The nurse who'd taken charge turned around and hollered to Kyle. "Have a seat in the waiting room, and I'll come get you once we get her settled."

"But I don't know *her…*" he started to say, but they disappeared into a room.

He yawned and walked slowly toward the room she'd pointed to, his spirits lifting when he spotted the coffee station in the corner. He dispensed a large cup from the tall thermal decanter and then peeled back the lid of four creamers, dumping them in and stirring with a thin, red swizzle straw.

Lifting the steaming coffee to his lips, he sipped the hot liquid and cradled the cup with both hands to warm himself up. He glanced at the clock, having no idea of the time, staring in disbelief that it was four o'clock in the morning. No wonder he was exhausted.

Kyle lowered his tired bones down onto one of the chairs in the waiting room, unable to stop thinking about what the old woman had said to him. Who was she? She acted like she knew him, but he had no idea who she was. Did Caleb know? Or perhaps Old Man Yoder knew her. She'd warned him to get away from the place before it was too late. Too late for what?

The thing that nagged at him the most, was the fact she'd called him *son*. Did she really think he was her son? Perhaps she had a family out there somewhere that was missing her. Certainly it wasn't him or Caleb; both their mothers were long-since dead. But they'd recently discovered

Amelia's mom alive when they'd thought she was dead too!

Kyle shook away the crazy thought. It was either too late at night or too early in the morning for that type of crazy thought, and he wasn't sure which one. It was one of those for sure, but he refused to entertain the thought again.

He'd attended his mother's funeral. He'd seen her body in the casket, and he'd never forget how cold and stiff she was, and how she just didn't look anything like herself. The life had gone from her, and she was nothing like the woman he'd known in his youth.

Sadly, they weren't particularly close in her last years, and he'd found himself regretting that as an adult. The woman certainly had her secrets. She seemed to have a whole other life that he knew nothing about. It was so full of mystery, and whatever it was, had caused her great pain.

He would always regret leaving home at the age of ten, but he'd found it too difficult to relate to his mother, and it'd been easier on him to stay with his uncle's family. His uncle didn't ask questions, and he didn't make any rules. What young boy wouldn't like that? Kyle certainly did. Suddenly, he was his own man, and he didn't have anyone to worry about, except himself. No more making sure his mother was dressed to go to the bank to cash her welfare check so they could eat. No more having to cut classes when the landlady would complain his mother was sitting outside on the front stoop in her bathrobe in the dead of winter.

Truth-be-told, this woman reminded him so much of his own mother, it scared him.

Kyle had too often regretted not growing up a little faster and taking on the responsibility God had dropped in his lap where his mother was concerned, but at ten years old, he was incapable of understanding the responsibility of caring for her. Not only was he too young, he'd become tired of having to be the parent, especially when the only time his mother seemed lucid was when she went on her special outings twice a week.

He'd seen his mother quite often just after he'd moved out, but as time wore on, she'd fallen into a deeper and deeper depression, and had even stopped going on her outings. He just couldn't understand her life at such an early age, and as a result, he didn't see her very often after that.

Her death had come as a shock to him, and he regretted not being with her when she died. After her funeral, he'd had no other choice but to be raised for the last four years of his childhood by his mother's brother. It had taken his mother's death to realize that she and her brother weren't even close, which made it easier for Kyle to stay away.

Now, twelve years later, the memories still haunted him.

If only he'd been there for her.

The nurse entered the waiting room and Kyle looked up at her.

"Your mother needs you," she said.

Kyle looked behind him at the row of chairs, but he was the only one in the room.

"If you're talking about the woman I brought in here," he said. "She's not my mother."

"I'm sorry, Sir, but she told us you were her son. She called you her son, and I guess we just assumed."

"I don't know who she is," he said. "But I aim to find out."

Kyle followed the nurse into the room, and thankfully, the woman was resting peacefully. He looked at all the tubes and wires attached to her, and the IV that would hydrate her again. Perhaps then she would begin to make some sense. He watched the monitor above the head of the bed, thinking that her heart rate seemed pretty normal.

"Hello son," the woman said, startling Kyle.

He looked at her for a moment, studying her face, but it was not familiar to him. Was she the one who was confused, or was it him? If it was her, he certainly didn't want to hurt her after all she'd been through. Did he have the heart to let her down easily?

He had to.

"You do know I'm not your son, don't you?" Kyle asked.

"How can you be sure of this?" she asked.

"Because I buried my mother some years ago," he said, his eyes down-cast.

"I see," she said quietly.

"Do you know what your name is?" he asked nervously.

"I don't think I'm going to tell you that."

"You know they have you listed here as Jane Doe, right?"

"I kind of like that name," she said.

"You need to know they won't let you out of here until they find out who you are," Kyle said. "I think you deserve to know that."

"But I have to get out of here!" she said with a sense of urgency that worried Kyle all over again.

"I don't want them to hold me here," she said. "Will you tell them I'm your mother?"

"I don't know that I want to lie for you unless there's a reason, and it better be a good reason."

She looked at him soberly, her eyes getting misty.

"Come on now, I don't want you getting all upset," Kyle said, feeling bad for her. "I just want to know what you were doing out there by the Yoder's barn in the middle of the night—without a jacket or shoes!"

She looked away, her jaw clenched, and she swallowed hard. Kyle could see that something was upsetting her. He also sensed she didn't want to tell him.

"I think you know you can trust me," he said. "I brought you here."

She turned to look at him, taking into consideration the sincerity in his eyes. She had to trust someone. If she was wrong, she would end up right back in captivity, but she knew she had to take a chance.

"Why should I trust you?"

Kyle sighed heavily. "Let's just say I owe it to my real mom."

"But you said your mother was dead," she replied.

"That has a lot to do with the fact that I let her down," he said soberly.

Her look softened. "I find that hard to believe," the old woman said. "You brought me here, and you helped me when you didn't have to. You could have left me out there to die."

Kyle smirked. "I suppose that's because I've done a lot of growing up since then."

She looked at him with seriousness in her eyes, a sense of urgency in her voice. "I need to get out of here immediately."

"Well, you're not going anywhere until they hydrate you. And I suppose I'm going to have to get you some shoes and a coat. Do you know where I can find any of that?"

She shook her head and wouldn't look at him.

Kyle sat down on the edge of the bed and took her hand in his. "If I'm going to help you, I need to know one thing," he said. "Were you breaking into the barn, or out of it?"

Her lower lip trembled, and the beeping of the heart monitor sped up.

"I'm not going to hurt you," Kyle said. "I only want to help. Were you breaking into the barn, or out?"

She parted her lips to speak, but hesitated, looking up into Kyles trusting eyes.

"Out," she whispered. "I was breaking out!"

Chapter 4

Kyle watched and waited for old man Yoder to drive his buggy out onto the main road before getting out of his truck and heading toward the man's barn. He just had to get in there and see if he could find any evidence that might shed some light on the truth about the mysterious woman. She'd refused to tell him who she was, but he had a hunch about her identity, and wouldn't know for sure unless he checked out the barn.

Knowing the only way he would find out was to go back to the scene where he'd found her, he would reluctantly investigate on his own. Not wanting to cause a stir and alert old man Yoder of his presence, he decided to walk down to the barn. The way he figured, his getaway would be easier on foot if the old man decided to come back.

As he walked out into the cornfield, stepping over the brown stalks that were nubs sticking up from the frozen earth, he wondered how Caleb would feel about him checking up on his dad. He knew the two of them were not close, so he reasoned that it was best for the sake of the woman to see if there was some truth to her story.

He walked slowly, keeping an eye over his shoulder for any sign he wasn't alone on the path. Even in the light of day, Kyle could feel his stomach churning at the thought of going near the Yoder's barn behind the old man's back— especially if he had been, in any way, holding the mysterious woman against her will as she'd suggested.

When he approached the barn, he noticed there was something different. The downed fence had been repaired, and the large generator that electrified it was gone.

It had snowed heavily from the time Kyle had taken the woman to the hospital up to now, and it covered over a lot, including the spot where the woman's body had laid in the snow.

Backing up to get a better look, he stepped on a twig, and the noise echoed loudly enough to make him jump. He took in a deep breath, chiding himself for suddenly being afraid of his own shadow. He had to keep his head if he was going to get through this.

Grabbing a long stick that had fallen from the tree, Kyle tossed it at the fence, cringing, until it hit the wires. Expecting to see sparks fly, he was surprised when nothing happened. Strangely, the fence was no longer electrified.

His gaze followed the span of the fence line, realizing the only way he was getting anywhere near the Yoder's barn would be to climb over the fence or break through it—neither of which would be an easy task.

Sizing up the fairly large tree in front of him, he decided to climb it and jump from the limb that extended over the fence line.

Kyle made quick work of shimmying up the tree, extended himself out onto the branch, and dropped onto the property, before thinking of how he was going to get back out of the enclosure.

I'll have to worry about that later, he said, blowing out a heavy sigh.

Checking around to be sure there was no one around, he slowly approached the barn. His heart sped up as he opened the barn door, thinking to himself he had no way of protecting himself should the need arise. He had not completely thought this through, and if the woman was truly in danger here, it could mean he was in danger as well. He closed the barn door behind him, scanning the unusually clean barn, looking for any shred of evidence that the woman had been there.

He walked slowly toward the tack-room, remembering what Amelia had told him about the Derringer being hidden under the work-bench in there. He didn't hold much hope that it would still be there, but he knew he'd feel better having it in his possession.

Crouching down, Kyle felt around under the bench until his outstretched fingers connected with a metal box. He pulled it toward him, and it was just as she'd described. He opened the lid, but found only a few stray bullets mixed with dirty straw.

That's funny, he thought, as he held one of the bullets up to examine it. *This is a 41 short, Rim-fire.*

It made sense to him, having a considerable amount of knowledge about guns, that it was one of the bullets that were loaded in the Derringer. He'd also read the coroner's report that listed the bullet that was extracted from his father's body, and he could've sworn the bullet that killed him was listed as a 41 long.

Making a mental note to check over the documents that he knew were tucked away in a box somewhere, he put the thought away for the time-being and stuffed one of the bullets into his pocket, then, replaced the box under the workbench.

Checking to be sure he was the only one in the barn, he listened intently until he was sure there were no noises other than his own. Standing up, he walked toward the back of the barn, when his eyes caught a flicker from a crossbeam of the rafters. The bright reflection of the winter sun streaming into the small window reflected off something shiny up there. From the barn floor he could not see exactly what the tiny object was, but he had to admit the shiny object piqued his curiosity.

Pulling out his phone, he opened up the camera on it, and then zoomed in to focus in on the object. His eyes darted from his phone screen to the cross beam, and back again, surprised to see that the object looked just like the bullet that was tucked away in his pocket.

Now he *had* to go up there to see exactly what it was. How could he let something that curious slip through his fingers? He snapped a few pictures and then stuffed his phone back into his pocket.

Climbing the ladder to the loft, Kyle walked over to where the object was wedged in the crossbeam and leaned over the edge to get a better look. Reaching down, he realized that it was indeed a bullet that matched the one he put in his pocket.

He wondered how it would've gotten there. Was it possible that was the bullet that dislodged from the gun the night Amelia shot Bruce? If that was the case, that would mean that someone else had killed his father.

He remembered hearing from Caleb and Amelia that the only place they had shot the gun was out in the field, using tin cans for practice. Surely no one would shoot the gun in such a closed space like this, with the exception being the night that Bruce was shot.

Knowing it was eight years ago and Amelia was just a child when it happened, he was eager to talk to her and ask her about the possibility of another shot being fired that night. For now, he needed to check out the rest of the barn before Old Man Yoder showed up. He left the bullet where it was, assuming he had been the only one to notice it there. He knew if he removed something that could be considered evidence, it could hurt the case if there was to be an additional investigation.

Again, he pulled his cell phone from his pocket, and took several pictures of the bullet where it was lodged in the cross beam, as opposed to removing it and risking tampering with possible evidence.

Kyle jumped down from the loft, his feet landing on the fresh straw on the floor, making a hollow sound rather than a solid one. Was it possible there was a space beneath the barn? He swished the straw with his feet, unearthing a small trapdoor.

His heart skipped a beat.

Why does there always have to be a trap door or a secret room? he asked himself half-jokingly.

This was the kind of thing scary movies were made of, and it set his nerves on edge. He looked around once more to be sure he was alone in the barn, relief washing over him when he was satisfied he was still the only one in the barn.

I need to get ahold of myself before I scare myself to death, he chided himself.

He took a deep breath and lifted the latch. He sucked in his breath upon seeing the ladder that led down into a dark room below ground.

Did he dare go down there?

It was obvious that Old Man Yoder was hiding something, and that made him nervous, but he knew if he didn't keep looking, he'd never find the answers he sought.

Grabbing a lantern from one of the support beams, where it hung from a nail, he lit a match from the little tin box that was nailed to the pole. He lit the lantern and crouched down on his haunches, lowering the lantern into the space, illuminating the room below.

It was certainly creepy, to say the least, but no matter how nervous it made him, he had to push from his mind the thoughts that filled him with so much terror, it made the hair raise off the back of his neck.

He shuddered at the thought of going down there, but forced himself to grab the lantern and lower himself down the ladder. When his feet connected with the dirt floor, he held up the lantern, turning all the way around and looking around the strange empty room. There was nothing but a dirt floor and four cinderblock walls. There was nothing in the room whatsoever, and strangely, not even cobwebs.

Fear crept back up his spine, feeling suddenly spooked. The last thing he needed or wanted was to be trapped in this room. He took one last look at the dirty walls that suddenly seemed to be closing in on him. His legs felt wobbly, and his breathing hitched at a noise from up above. His heart slammed against his ribcage when the latch door shut with a loud crash.

"Oh, God," he said with a heaving breath. "Don't let me be trapped in here!"

His legs felt weak when he heard footsteps on the floor above his head. The old man knew he was there!

His nerves jangling, he backed away from the trapdoor, looking around the room again for *anything* he could use to defend himself. In the far corner, he found a thick piece of glass that looked like it had come from a broken Mason jar. He held it up to the light, examining what looked like dried blood on it.

He dropped it to the ground. "I *have* to get out of here!" he said, not realizing how loud he was being.

The footfalls above him faded, and the barn door closed. Had the old man left, or was it a trick?

Kyle waited and listened, his eyes bulging in the dark cellar. How long did he have to wait before it was safe to try the latch? His mind reeled with the possibility that it wouldn't open, and he'd be trapped indefinitely.

"Lord, I know I don't talk to you as often as I should, but right now I pray you'll forgive me for that, and help me out of here. I'm scared!"

His prayer surprised him, but he had exhausted his own means of trying to stay calm. He needed a higher power to help. His faith was weak, but Amelia and Caleb had told him that was when God was there the most.

"I pray you were right, my friends," he said of Caleb and Amelia.

When several minutes had passed, and all was still silent, Kyle decided to try the trapdoor. Looping the lantern over his forearm, he climbed the ladder and pushed at the heavy, wooden door, but it wouldn't open.

Panic filled him as he slammed his shoulder against it repeatedly, grunting and pushing with everything he had in him. Working up a sweat, the latch began to wiggle loose, but Kyle kept heaving his weight against it over and over until it finally popped open.

Taking in a deep breath, he raised his head above the floor level just enough to look around the barn for signs of the old man. When he didn't see him, he hoisted himself up as fast as he could and slammed the lid shut.

After closing the latch, he quickly raked the straw back over the door, snuffed out the lantern and replaced it on its nail on the pole.

Listening for noises, Kyle had an uneasy feeling, but couldn't get out of that barn fast enough. He hurried out the door and made a running jump for the tree branch that hung over the fence line, adrenalin his driving force, he grabbed onto the limb on the first try. Hurling his legs up using every muscle in his abdomen, he shimmied back down the branch onto the tree trunk.

When his feet hit the ground, he took off running back through the open field, feeling vulnerable until he reached the *dawdi haus*.

He rushed into the door out of breath and leaned against the frame to steady his wobbly legs. His breathing was so labored he felt he couldn't get enough air. He walked over to the sink and looked out the kitchen window. Was the old man really someone to be afraid of, or had he been closed in the cellar by accident?

Pouring himself a cup of coffee with a shaky hand, he wasn't sure if finding nothing was good or bad, but he didn't intend to go back there again.

He knew he needed something to collaborate the old woman's story, but it wasn't worth all of this. What was it that the old man was hiding, and what did it have to do with that woman? Had she been a part of the bank robbery? The old man had come clean with his part in it, but not before he used pig blood to scare Amelia. Was he capable of much worse? Things that even his own son had no knowledge of?

Kyle shuddered at the thought of returning to the hospital empty-handed and with no answers to give her. He also knew he would be hard-pressed to get any more information out of her, and that discouraged him. He needed answers.

He was no closer to figuring out who she was, and she wasn't giving him the answers he needed.

Perhaps now was the time for him to rethink his involvement.

Chapter 5

"What do you mean she's in the psychiatric ward?" Kyle asked, raking his hands through his thick hair. "How could you put my mother in such a place?"

The nurse looked at him and raised an eyebrow. "You told us last night you had no idea who she was, and now she's your mother suddenly?"

He hadn't meant to say that, but he thought perhaps it might help to get him in to see her. He needed to see her like he needed his next breath. She was the only one that could provide the answers he needed, and she was also the only one who could tell him if he was in danger. Certain that only family members would get in to see her in the psychiatric ward, he hoped he could convince the nurse enough to allow a visit with the old woman.

"I'm sorry, Sir," the nurse said. "But we found drugs in her bloodstream when we did the blood-work, and she became hysterical about an hour ago, screaming and rambling on that there was a man in her room who was trying to kill her, but when we looked, there was no one there."

Kyle had a hunch he knew who it was.

"What kind of drugs?" he asked.

"I'm sorry, but unless you can provide proof that she's your blood relative, we aren't at liberty to give you that information, because right now she's registered here as Jane Doe, and she'll stay that way until you can provide some ID for her. Until you can get that information for us, we're required to keep her privacy."

Kyle knew he didn't have any such thing, but he hoped that he could gain the sympathy of the nursing staff. If not, there was no way he would be able to help her.

"Did she describe the man she claims was trying to kill her?"

"She said he was her husband," the nurse said.

Kyle's blood went cold and he stumbled backward against the wall. He felt like he couldn't breathe.

"Are you alright?" the nurse asked.

He nodded.

It was obvious to Kyle that Old Man Yoder had been at the hospital and had paid the woman a visit, but now he knew the woman had to be Caleb's mother—his dead mother.

"Is it possible for me to visit her?"

The nurse sighed. "I don't see how it could hurt. After all, you're the only one that she seems to know, and she certainly looked comfortable with you. If you can help her put the pieces of her life back together, that would be the best thing for her.

She's very confused. If you happen to upset her, we'll have to ask you to leave."

"I'll do my best," Kyle promised. "Please let me see her; I need to talk to her."

Kyle felt sick to his stomach. If she was truly Caleb's mother, he wondered how he would react when he found out. He'd described to Kyle how his father had *lost his mind* after being shunned from the community, but was a shunned Amish man really capable of all of this? Keeping a person—even a spouse, locked up was a crime, wasn't it?

There was no denying the old man was in the barn earlier and had closed the latch on the cellar door while Kyle was down there, but how did he manage to get to the hospital and back so fast?

So, he still had a few details to work out, but if it was not the old man who was here threatening her, who was it? One thing was certain; if the old woman was *frau* Yoder, he would have to believe her story.

If Old Man Yoder had been holding her down in the cellar against her will, he'd certainly done a fine job of cleaning up all the evidence, and Kyle would be hard-pressed to prove any of it. Still, he'd seen the two large generators he'd used to power the electric fence, but now they were gone, so perhaps he'd cleaned up all of her belongings while he was at it. Since she'd escaped, he'd have to hide the evidence—but where?

Kyle could not quiet his thoughts as he followed the nurse to the elevator.

Maybe it was best to report all of this and let the authorities handle it. But before he got the police involved, he wanted to talk to the old woman one more time.

The nurse led Kyle up to the third-floor, and into a locked-down area, and then to a room where she used her ID badge to open the locked door. Behind that door was the old woman, and she was resting quietly on the bed by the window staring blankly out the window

"What's wrong with her?" Kyle whispered to the nurse.

"We had to give her a mild sedative to calm her down. Like I said, she was just hysterical and screaming. You could hear her all the way down the hall. We put her in here for her own safety— on the off-chance that someone really was in the room with her. We've put in a call to the sheriff's department. They should be sending an officer soon."

Now his need to talk to her was even more urgent. He wanted to find out as much as he could before she talked to any police.

"Did you have to call them?" he asked.

"Since she has no idea who she is, or at least she isn't giving us any real clues except saying it was her husband in here earlier harassing her, we're required to file a missing person search. That way, if she has any family, they can come and claim her."

"But I told you *I'm* her family," Kyle said.

"I know what you said, young man, but I have to wonder what you're trying to protect her from."

"I'm not exactly sure yet," he admitted. "But I'm trying to find out."

"I know you mean well," the nurse said. "But maybe you should just let the police handle it. They do this all the time. They can protect her."

"They weren't there to protect her when I found her. I feel responsible. I have a feeling she's the mother of an Amish friend of mine."

"Amish?" she asked. "That would make sense. I can tell she's trying to hide her accent, but I can still detect it. I have a friend who's Amish, and I've come to know the way they sound. She sounds Amish—but kind of like she's trying to hide it!"

Kyle felt very sorry for the woman, realizing that it was possible she was beyond his reach, and beyond his capabilities to help her, but he would certainly do his best to try.

Chapter 6

Kyle looked at his watch as he outstretched his arms and yawned. Jerking his arm up to his face, he stared at the clock face one more time. It was almost 6 o'clock.

"Greta!" he said aloud. "How could I have forgotten about my buggy ride with Greta?"

He stepped off the elevator and walked down the long corridor. How was he going to be able to enjoy his time with Greta when he had so much weighing on his mind? Caleb had gone out of his way to introduce the two of them after Kyle had seen her on a couple of occasions when they were visiting with his cousins, and had become immediately infatuated with her. Caleb had managed to convince his older cousin to talk his neighbor into going out with Kyle, even though he was an *Englisher*.

He looked at his watch again, worrying. "If I hurry, I'll have just enough time to get back to shower and get ready for my date."

Before long, he was pulling the truck into the long drive to Caleb's and Amelia's new house. He could see the Yoder's barn when he pulled up to the *dawdi haus,* and it made his heart thump a few extra beats. Just thinking about being stuck in that root cellar made him sick to his stomach.

He momentarily wondered if he should even continue to stay at his friends' house, even though he agreed to stay so he could feed the horses and the cats. He could certainly do that during the day and go back to his apartment despite the lengthy drive back and forth. It had been the only reason it made sense to stay at Caleb's farm. Maybe he would go back into town just until all this blew over, and he figured out what was really going on, and if he was truly in danger.

For now, he had to assume it was a coincidence that he got closed in the cellar, but it didn't seem like a coincidence that he found the old woman where he did. Hysteria over the possible visit from Old Man Yoder, however, was not something to push from his mind. But maybe it was someone else who'd visited her—or no one at all, as the hospital staff had suggested. Maybe, just maybe, he found a homeless, crazy old woman trying to break into the Yoder's barn, and there was nothing more to come of it than that.

It frustrated him that his visit with the old woman had not gone well. Not only was she not completely awake from the medicine that made her groggy, but she certainly was not willing to give him any personal information that would prove her identity. So, for the time being, perhaps the nurse was correct in saying she was safer in a locked-down facility. It was possible she was a danger even to herself.

He hated leaving her, but the medicine had finally won, and she'd fallen into a deep and fitful sleep. He'd listened for a little while until she'd gone deeper into sleep, but while she was having nightmares it seemed she was deeply disturbed over something, and he could only make out a few words she'd mumbled in her sleep, but she'd said the same thing repeatedly; she kept saying she was sorry—to her son. Was it possible she had a son out there somewhere that was missing her? It even crossed his mind that the son could be Caleb.

Kyle stepped out of the truck, looking all around Caleb's farm, feeling suddenly very uneasy about being there. He would decide what to do about his living arrangement later. For now, he didn't want to be late for his first date. He really liked Greta, and he didn't want to mess this up. He felt lucky that she was willing to give him a chance, even though she'd mentioned his only fault was that he was an *Englisher!* He couldn't do anything to change the fact he was an *Englisher,* so he wouldn't chance ruining what might possibly be his only chance with her by being late. It was already bad enough that his mind was not on this date, and he would have a hard time keeping it there. If not for his extreme attraction to her and the fact he already felt he was falling for her, he would have rescheduled the date.

Kyle quickly cleaned himself up and put on the plain clothes that Caleb had suggested. He wanted to appear as Amish as possible. It wasn't that he was trying to change himself, but rather adapt to something that she was used to. Besides, if he could do anything else to appeal to her, it would be worth it to him. He felt a little odd wearing a pair of black dress pants and a navy dress shirt, but he had to admit he did look really nice, and the shirt complimented his blue eyes.

He certainly hoped she would find him appealing. Caleb had been kind enough to teach him how to hitch up the buggy to his horse, Chestnut. He and his bride had taken a Greyhound bus to Florida for their non-traditional honeymoon.

Kyle and Chestnut had gotten to know each other over the past week while he'd been there feeding him. Kyle was rather enjoying the horse's company. He was especially grateful for how cooperative the horse was when he was trying to hitch him to the buggy.

Once everything was fastened down, Kyle hopped up into the buggy, making sure he had enough lap quilts, and then picked up the reins and prompted Chestnut down the long driveway. He was so proud of himself for learning how to drive the buggy, and he hoped that Greta would look upon him fondly because of it.

Kyle steered Chestnut down the snowy Lane, feeling grateful he didn't have to drive the buggy far. He felt confident taking the horse down the quiet country road, knowing the likelihood of running into any cars was next to none. Even if he did, it was a straight, flat road, and he could see for miles. Drivers would be able to spot him easily, and that made him confident that his risk was minimal. It wasn't that he didn't trust the horse or his own ability to drive, but he'd seen too many haphazard drivers not being careful around the buggies, or drivers getting impatient around them, which seemed to cause a lot of accidents.

When he pulled up the lane to Greta's house, he was happy to see that she was waiting on the covered porch for him, on the porch swing. Her smile warmed his heart as she bound from the swing and down the steps to the driveway to greet him.

Kyle hopped down from the buggy and assisted Greta up; the warmth of her hand making his skin tingle. She'd removed her mitten to take his hand, and he had removed his glove. He couldn't help feeling her hand fit his perfectly.

Climbing up into the buggy, Kyle sat close to her and spread the lap quilt across both of their laps, feeling another tingle down his spine when their thighs touched. They rode in silence down the driveway, and out to the main road. It was a pleasant sort of quiet, but Kyle enjoyed the sound of her voice, and hoped he could mask his nervousness by getting her to talk. He was certain that, like most females, once she got to talking, she wouldn't likely stop, and that would ease the first-date tension a little. At least, he hoped it would.

"Tell me," Kyle said trying to steady his voice. "How long have you known Caleb and Amelia?"

Greta giggled. "We grew up together in the community, so I've known them both since we were born—with the exception of the time Amelia has been gone. But even then, we weren't supposed to see either of them after the shunning. But since two of his cousins are still in their *rumspringa,* they can see him. I can too, since I'm in my *rumspringa* too. It's really the only reason I can take this buggy ride with you—since you're an *Englisher."*

"What is it like to have to shun people in the community? Does it happen a lot?"

"Not as often as most *Englishers* think it does."

"I'm not sure if being shunned has been good for Caleb or his dad."

"His *daed* has always been a strange man," she said.

Kyle chuckled. "He seems very angry."

"Before *Frau* Yoder died, he'd pulled away from the community. He stayed away, and we didn't see much of Caleb, and neither did my brothers, and they were all friends. Then, after everything happened with Amelia and the shooting, they were shunned, but I overheard *mei daed* saying to *mei mamm* that Zeb Yoder had gotten a little *narrish*—crazy. He said the man was not the same after his wife died, but some say he was not right since they were young—after he came back from his *rumspringa*."

Suddenly, Kyle had a million questions, but didn't want to worry Greta with all of them, so he picked only one.

"What was Caleb's mother's given name?"

"I don't know. The community would have referred to her as *Frau Yoder*, and I don't remember her, so I would have no idea." Greta said sadly. "I know she had an older *schweschder*. I don't think Caleb ever met his *mamm's schweschder*. I heard she left the community when she was on her *rumspringa,* and she never came back. There were rumors that she had a *boppli*—

baby, out of wedlock, but no one knows for sure, or has ever seen her since."

"What was her sister's name?" he asked.

"I don't know that either. I really don't know that much, and can't offer more than I've already told you."

"I'm sorry for bringing it all up," he said. "I just don't know much about Caleb, other than the fact that our parents were involved somehow all those years ago, and I just had a bit of a run-in with his dad."

"What kind of a run-in?"

Kyle patted her hand. "It's not important. Let's enjoy the snowy night. Would you like to go down to the pond and look at the moon?"

Greta smiled. "I'd like that very much."

Even though Greta's information shed some light on a few things for him, it wasn't anything he could use to help solve the mystery woman's identity—unless she was *Frau Yoder*. For now, he would put all of that behind him, and concentrate on the lovely Greta, his Amish date.

Kyle steered the buggy down the gravel road toward the pond that overlooked the Yoder's property. From that distance, he could see the lanterns being lit on the sides of the old man's buggy.

Where would he be going at this time of night?

Kyle wasn't going to worry about it. He turned his attention to his date. Tonight was his night, and he was not going to let Old Man Yoder or the mystery woman spoil it for him.

"Did you know you have the same color eyes as Caleb?" Greta said. "When I first met you, I thought you were a relative of his."

Kyle chuckled. "You think we look alike?"

She smiled. "*Jah.*"

"They say everyone in the world has a *twin—or a double*—someone who looks so much like them that people say they must be twins from another lifetime. What is the word for it? Oh yeah—it's called *doppelganger,* but I don't think we look that much alike."

"I do!" she said. "Especially in that hat!"

Kyle swiped Caleb's black hat off his head, feeling a little embarrassed that he'd worn it. Caleb had told him it would make his *date* a little easier on Greta, but it seems he'd only made a fool of himself.

Greta took the hat from him and placed it back on his head. "I like that hat. It suits you. I almost forgot you weren't Amish for a minute."

"I can't make myself Amish," he said. "But I'm willing to dress this way if it makes it easier for you."

"I want you to be yourself. I like you despite the fact you're an *Englisher.*"

He chuckled. "I'm not sure if I should take that as a compliment."

She cozied up to him and looked him in the eye. "You can!"

They continued to talk, but about the weather, and what it was like for her growing up Amish. He could have listened to her talk all night, and the more she talked, the more he fell in love with her.

The bright light of the full moon shining on her pink cheeks made him forget everything except what was right in front of him. He wanted more than anything to kiss her, but he feared her reaction.

Kyle blinked away snowflakes from his lashes, suddenly throwing caution to the wind as he bent toward her and pressed his lips gently to hers. Surprisingly, she deepened the kiss, but she let out a little shiver.

"I should take you home," he said as he pulled gently away from her soft lips. "We've been out here for hours, and the wind is really picking up."

She moved in closer, and he wrapped his arms around her.

"I'm not too cold to end the evening," she said. "But it is getting late. I want to be able to see you again, and *mei daed* won't like you if you don't bring me home at a respectable hour."

Kyle smiled. She wanted to see him again, and he couldn't be happier. "I'd like to see you again too."

She pressed her lips to his, and this time, he pulled her close, kissing her like a man in love.

Kyle left Greta's driveway feeling happier than he thought he could. He'd forgotten all about his troubles with Old Man Yoder and the mystery woman, and could think of nothing except his date and the feel of her lips on his. He puckered his lips against the cold air, happy that they still tingled with warmth from hers.

Pulling the buggy up to Caleb's barn, he talked to Chestnut. "I'm sure you'll be happy to get back into the barn and see your new sweetheart too!" he said to him.

Caleb had purchased a mare for Amelia for a wedding gift, and even though Chestnut would not be able to mate with her, being a gelding, he still seemed to take a liking to her.

After rubbing him down and putting a blanket on him for the night, Kyle shouldered out into the wind toward the *dawdi haus,* when he noticed the door was open and the lights were on. How had he missed that when he'd pulled up, or had someone gone in the house while he was in the barn for the past half hour?

He walked cautiously toward his truck, pulling a crow bar from his toolbox across the bed. If someone was in the house, what would he do? A crowbar was not something to defend yourself with! The only thing he couldn't figure out was that there wasn't a vehicle around, and there were no fresh tire tracks—only the tracks from Caleb's buggy.

As he neared the porch, he noticed large footprints—likely from a man, that led into the kitchen. He stood at the door and listened. The puddles of water left would indicate the person had gone inside the house a while ago since the snow had melted, but there was something else.

Blood!

He cautiously stepped up to the doorway, shaking, and wondering if he shouldn't call the police instead of going into the home alone. He would feel like a fool if it turned out to be nothing, but if someone was hurt in there, they would need help.

He took a deep breath, and held the crowbar over his head, ready to strike at the first sign of trouble, and walked slowly, following the wet puddles and blood splatters to the small bathroom off the kitchen. He froze when he looked up into the mirror and saw the words painted on the mirror in blood that served as a warning to him:

Leave this place!

Kyle jumped and turned on his heels at a noise behind him, the crowbar raised. Walking slowly toward the kitchen, his heart racing, he kept the crowbar up and ready to swing at whatever was out there. Before he could even think about it, he felt a blow to the back of his head, and he was falling to the floor. The crowbar clanged when it hit the floor just before he did, and his last thought just before everything went black, was of the old woman and her warning to leave.

Chapter 7

Kyle tried to lift his face up from the linoleum floor, but he couldn't even move. His lashes fluttered as he focused on a large pair of boots standing in front of his face. There was someone there with him, but he couldn't get up.

"Bring her back," a gruff voice said to him. "Or you'll replace her!"

Kyle groaned as he closed his eyes against the pain in his head. He listened to the foot-falls fade as the person walked out of the house, but he was too weak to open his eyes to see who it was, but he had his hunches. He knew it could only be one person; Old Man Yoder.

Sometime later, Kyle's eyes opened slightly, the bright sun from the kitchen window warming his face. How had morning managed to come without him realizing? Had he been asleep on the floor the entire night? He groaned as he tried to move, the pain in his head quite intense.

Reaching back with his hand, he felt something warm, moist and sticky. Bringing his hand back down in front of his face, he could see that his fingers were bloody. He could barely move, but he needed help. Rolling on his side slowly, he cringed against the pain in his head, as he struggled to remember what had happened.

Pushing himself up, Kyle rested his back against the cupboards, unable to stand up just yet. He felt dizzy, and sick to his stomach, but he was awake enough to know he needed help. Reaching into his pocket, he grabbed his cell phone and dialed 911.

"911, what's your emergency?" the person on the other end asked.

"I—I think I need an ambulance," Kyle said. "And maybe a police officer."

"What's the nature of your injury?" the person asked.

"I've been hit on the head, and my head is bleeding."

"What's your address?"

"I'm at, um, 25925 County Road 17, Pigeon Hollow," he said, trying to remember Caleb's address.

"Is there someone with you?"

"No, I'm here alone. Someone hit me last night, and I've been passed out all this time."

"Was it a male or female that struck you?"

"I'm pretty sure it was a man."

"Do you happen to know the person who hit you?"

"I can't prove it, but I have an idea," he said.

"Did you see the person's face? Can you identify him?"

Kyle thought about the pair of boots he saw, and realized he never actually saw the person who'd hit him.

"No, I didn't see his face. I was lying on the floor and only saw his boots."

"I have an officer and an ambulance on the way. Do you want me to stay on the phone with you until they get there?"

"I don't know," Kyle said. "I think I'm gonna be sick."

"I'll stay on the line with you, but you can put the phone down if you need to."

Kyle agreed, but he couldn't hold the phone to his ear any longer. He let his hand fall to his lap, his phone fell to the floor, and his eyes drifted closed a few times as he fought off the urge to vomit.

Within a few minutes, he heard sirens off in the distance and prayed they would get to him in time.

Before he realized, Kyle was being put on a stretcher and he woke up just slightly.

"Can you hear me?" a paramedic was asking him.

Kyle reached up and pulled the oxygen mask off his face so he could speak. "The mirror," he said weakly. "He painted a warning on the bathroom mirror—in blood."

The police officer approached him. "What are you talking about, young man?"

"Look at the mirror in the bathroom. He painted a warning to me in blood."

The officer held up a finger to the paramedics to wait just a minute while he checked out the bathroom.

Kyle turned his head and watched the officer walk down the hall and turn on the bathroom light. He stood there for a minute, but then came back.

"What are you talking about?"

"The writing on the bathroom mirror," Kyle insisted. "He wrote it in blood."

"Who did?" he asked Kyle.

"The man who hit me!"

"There's nothing there, young man," the officer said. "You must've hit your head harder than you think. Were you drinking?"

"Drinking? No!" Kyle said. "I don't drink. "I'm telling you, someone hit me in the head, and it was the same person who wrote the warning on the bathroom mirror."

"What did the warning say?" the officer asked.

"It said: Leave this place."

"I'm sorry, Son," the officer said. "But there's no writing on the mirror, and there isn't any blood anywhere that I could see. Where this chair is on the kitchen floor, it looks like you fell. You probably hit your head then. There's a half-empty bottle of vodka on the kitchen table. How much of it did you drink?"

"I don't drink! That isn't mine!"

"Well the empty bottle and lack of evidence points toward you having a little too much to drink and a big imagination."

"But I'm telling you he hit me!" Kyle insisted. "He must've cleaned up the mess and put the bottle on the table after I passed out."

"I'm sorry, young man," the officer said. "But there's nothing here that indicates foul play, so I have no evidence to go by. If you had a witness, I'd have a case, but right now, I have nothing more than the word of a young kid who looks like he had a little too much to drink."

Kyle sighed and closed his eyes in defeat as the paramedic replaced the oxygen mask back over his face and wheeled him out to the ambulance.

Chapter 8

Kyle watched the nurse draw blood from his arm; blood he'd insisted they take from him to prove he wasn't drinking. The officer had accused him of such, and he aimed to prove he hadn't been. He was so confused right now and so groggy, that he was beginning to doubt himself, and he prayed this blood test would set his mind at ease.

They'd already stitched him up, and recommend he stay for twenty-four hours, but he only agreed to do that on the condition that they let him visit the woman who was upstairs in the locked-down facility. He hoped she might be able to solve the mystery of what had happened to him last night.

He needed to talk to her more than ever. He needed to find out if she was Caleb's mother. If she was, she perhaps, held the key to stopping Old Man Yoder from going completely off the deep end, though he feared it was too late to stop the inevitable. He knew he wasn't the one who was crazy, the old man was behind all of this, and Kyle was going to do everything in his power to prove it.

He had to admit, he found it odd that the warning written on the mirror was the same exact warning the old woman had given him. If not for the fact he knew she was in lockdown, he'd wonder if it was her that had done it. The fact remained, though, that Old Man Yoder already had a reputation for using blood as a scare-tactic.

After the blood he spread around Amelia's front door, and the rug in his own *dawdi haus*, this newest mischief had Old Man Yoder written all over it.

Only problem was, if it was only mischief, he wouldn't feel so threatened. Truth was, Kyle was terrified of the old man, and didn't intend on going back to Caleb's house except to feed the animals, and even then he would be on his guard.

No sooner did the nurse finish taking his blood, than he was out of the room and entering the elevator—before she had a chance to stop him.

Kyle approached the nurse's station, and asked them to let him in the old woman's room.

"I'm sorry, but she said she doesn't want to see you."

"I *have* to see her," he begged the nurses. "I know who she is!"

"You know who she is?" the nurse asked, turning to another nurse. "He says he knows who our Jane Doe is. Should I let him talk to her?"

"Tell us her name," the other nurse said.

"I have reason to believe she's my friend's mother. Her last name would be Yoder."

"Yoder?" the nurse asked. "So, she is Amish?"

"Yes, I believe so." Kyle answered.

"How did you figure this out?"

"Because I was just threatened by her husband, and I happen to be staying in her son's home. I'm a friend of his, and he's away on his honeymoon. He's thought his mother was dead for the past ten or so years."

"This just keeps getting better and better," one of the nurses said.

"You said her husband threatened you?" the nurse asked. "Did you tell the police?"

"Yes, I did," he said, showing them the stitches in the back of his head. "He hit me from behind and knocked me out, and while I was passed out, he cleaned up all the blood, and he put a bottle of vodka on the table to make it look like I was drunk. I had the nurses downstairs draw blood from me to prove I hadn't been drinking."

"Maybe we should wait to get the results of those tests," one of the nurses said. "Before we let you see her."

"Please," he begged. "I need to see her now. Please ask her if she'll see me. Tell her I know who she is. Well, maybe I should tell her that. She's going to be afraid when she finds out I know her identity. She knows her own name, I'm sure of it, but she isn't telling because she's afraid of the old man—her husband."

"I suppose it can't hurt to ask her if she'll see you," one of the nurses said.

She picked up the phone and dialed the woman's room, and after a minute or so, she asked the woman if she would see Kyle, then, briefly listened, and finally hung up the phone.

"She said she'll see you."

He let out the breath he'd been holding in, relieved she would see him, but he couldn't shake the bad feeling he had no matter what.

Following the nurse down the hall, he rehearsed in his mind what he might say to the woman, and how he would approach the subject of her name. Should he blurt it out, or address her by her real name when he entered, or should he wait for the right opportunity? He decided waiting would be best, and he'd have to bring it up delicately. The last thing he wanted to do was to spook her.

"You know the routine, right?" the nurse asked.

"Yes, I know, you have to lock me in with her. Would you mind standing outside the door, though—just in case."

The nurse raised an eyebrow. "Just in case of what?"

He sighed. "In case she doesn't take the news well and she needs to be medicated to calm her down!"

The nurse slid her key in the door and unlocked it, the woman sitting on the edge of the bed, facing the barred window.

"Hello, Mrs. Yoder," the nurse greeted her with a pasted-on smile. "I have a visitor for you!"

Kyle cringed, especially when he saw how disturbed the woman looked, her eyes suddenly very sad.

The nurse left the room and locked him in with her. Even though he knew she would be standing outside the door, he didn't like the idea of being locked in there with her. He didn't know her well enough to trust her, and after everything that had happened recently, he didn't trust anyone anymore—not even himself.

She glared at him as he sat in the chair in the corner of the room, and he tried to calm himself before speaking to her, knowing his voice would shake, giving away his fear.

"I'm sorry about that," he said as calmly and steadily as he could. "But they wouldn't let me in to see you unless I could identify you. Are you *Frau* Yoder?"

Her lower lip trembled and she looked out the window, feigning interest in the snow.

"No, I'm not *Frau* Yoder," she finally said. "But that's a good guess."

He didn't know whether to believe her or not, but decided to take another approach.

"Did you know *Frau* Yoder?" he asked cautiously.

"Yes, we were very close," she said soberly. "But now she's buried in my grave!"

Chapter 9

Kyle stirred a few times, falling in and out of the same dream. He felt a cold rag to his head, and the sound of his mother's angelic voice, as she sang the lullaby he hadn't heard since he was a child. He knew the foreign words by heart, and the tune played in his head as if haunting him, but he never knew what the words meant.

Unable to move, the pain in his head bound his eyelids closed as if by an invisible force, allowing him to dream. It was a dream he didn't want to wake from; a dream he would hold onto as long as he could, knowing once he woke, his mother would be gone, and he'd lose her all over again.

The pain in his head assaulted his skull like a wrecking ball. Perhaps he shouldn't have been so hasty in leaving the hospital, but he couldn't stay there after his disturbing talk with the old woman.

She'd become silent and restrained the moment she'd let the unspeakable escape her lips. The most confusing point was when he went to leave, and she suddenly asked to hug him—almost as if mourning the loss of her own son. If not for the fact he knew her embrace would satisfy his own mournful loss, he'd have rejected it altogether.

Kyle tossed about, the sound of his mother's voice drawing near, comforting him back to sleep, but only for a moment. Sleep would not stay, the pain too great to bear. He felt the spinning in his head like a clock wound too tightly, and bile threatened to spill from his throat. A cold sweat drenched him like the down-pouring of rain on a warm, summer night, but his mother was there to comfort him.

Had he driven home in this state? He reached with an outstretched arm for the familiar alarm clock at his bedside, pulling it close to his face, and

painfully lifting an eyelid just above a flutter to
see the time. The room was dark, but the red
numbers illuminated 4:27am. His hand relaxed on
the device, unable to move it back, but a gentle
hand swept it away, and then brought the cool rag
to his warm forehead.

Kyle groaned against the pain, but his mother's
comforting song lulled him just a little longer.
Sleep overcame him finally, and his mother's
gentle song left him.

Kyle woke to the distant sound of sirens, and as
the sound drew near, he could hear rustling at his
side.

"Get up, Kyle!" a woman's voice said. "I think the
police are here, and we need to get our story
straight!"

Kyle groaned, the pain in his head a little lighter
than it had been. He was groggy, and could hear
the sirens, but had thought he was dreaming them.

He tried to sit up, but he was still very dizzy. His mouth was dry and his eyes felt very heavy. He yawned and stretched, but the pain in his head kept him down flat on his back.

"Story?" Kyle asked as he focused on the old woman. "What? What are you doing here?"

"I brought you home yesterday, don't you remember?"

Kyle groaned as he wiped the sleep from his eyes and made another attempt to sit up.

"Do you even have a driver's license?"

She threw her hands up. "Not on me, no!"

He looked at her a little more closely, noting that she'd helped herself to his clothes. His sweat pants and t-shirt were baggy on her frail frame, but she looked a little healthier than the last time he'd seen her. In all fairness, anyone looked ill in a hospital gown.

"Did you break out of the mental ward at the hospital?"

She handed him a glass of water. "Not exactly. But we don't have time to discuss that right now."

"I won't go to jail for you!" Kyle said.

"No one is going to jail, but they could make me go back and I don't want to go back. It isn't safe there."

"It's not exactly safe here either! Or did you miss the sirens outside? I'm sure they brought an ambulance to take us *both* back! I broke out too!"

Hearing a car door, she jumped. "We need to tell them I'm your mother," she begged. "Please don't send me back there. It's just as bad as being locked in…"

She didn't finish her sentence, but Kyle had an idea what she was trying not to say.

"I've never lied to a police officer, but I'd be willing to bet it's against the law!"

"What if it's not a lie?"

He reached up and grabbed her arms and looked her in the eye, even though his vision was still a little blurry from sleep. The lump in his throat wouldn't let him speak until he swallowed it down.

"What do you mean, if it's not a lie?" he said, his eyes now wide with terror. "I went to your funeral!"

His heart raced, and his face felt like it was on fire. What was happening? Had he hit his head harder than he thought, and now he was dreaming this—or worse—was he dead?

"You might have gone to a funeral that day, but it wasn't mine!"

"I admit my mother didn't look right that day, but I hadn't seen her for a couple of years, and she'd been taking drugs, and…"

"No she wasn't!"

"How do you know this?"

"I don't have time to go into that right now. Just follow my lead, and we'll get rid of them."

Kyle shook as a knock sounded at the door.

"Can you *prove* you're my mother?"

"The only proof I have of anything is locked away in the attic at Zeb Yoder's house!"

Chapter 10

"We had a report ma'am, filed by Zebedee Yoder, and he states that you're his wife and that this young man is holding you against your will."

Selma practically choked on his words as she turned to Kyle. "*He's* not holding me against my will! I'm not that man's wife. There's a grave on the back of his land where his wife is buried. Perhaps you should ask him who's in that grave!" she challenged the officer. "Ask him if I'm his wife, then, who's in that grave. I can't very well be here standing in front of you, and be dead and buried at the same time, could I? Zeb Yoder is a very sick man. Perhaps you should turn your questions on him. As for me, I'm staying here with Kyle."

"She's my mother," he told the police officer, fully believing and praying she truly was. "I can vouch for her."

The officer tipped his hat and bid them goodbye.

After the police left, Kyle felt suddenly let down.

He turned to the woman, sadness rising up in him, causing his throat to constrict as he swallowed down tears. "You're Amish, aren't you?" he asked her.

"*Jah,* I'm Amish," she answered quietly.

He knew from her answer there was no way she was his mother, without even asking the question. He wouldn't ask her, because to do so would break his heart all over again.

Zeb looked up from hitching his horse to the buggy when two police cars pulled into his driveway. Searching for any sign that Selma was with them, he clenched his jaw and ground his teeth in anger. They were supposed to bring her back. After all, she belonged to him, and she didn't belong among the *English.*

"Good afternoon, I'm Officer Banks," the first officer said as he approached Zeb. "I understand you filed a missing person's report for your wife."

He clenched his jaw and looked at them sternly. "You were supposed to bring her back here! She belongs here with me."

"The woman says she isn't your wife, and she wants to stay where she is. I don't know what kind of domestic problems you're having, but we can't force a spouse to go back home if the person doesn't want to."

"This is not a matter for *Englishers* to decide. The Bishop decides, and she is *mei fraa."*

"Perhaps you could ask your *Bishop* to help you with this matter," the officer suggested.

Zeb narrowed his eyes. "I cannot. I'm shunned!" he said through gritted teeth.

"I'm afraid we can't help you," he said. "But we do have a couple of questions we'd like to ask."

Zeb glared at them, and then turned his back to them as he checked the harnesses on the buggy.

"She mentioned you have a grave on a family plot here on your property. Can you tell me whose grave it is? A *first* wife, perhaps?"

"The grave is empty!"

The officers gave each other a warning look.

"Empty?" Officer Banks asked. "Did you say the grave is empty?"

"*Jah,*" Zeb said without turning around. "This is none of your business. It is a *familye* matter."

"I'm afraid you're wrong about that, Mr. Yoder!" the officer said. "If we suspect foul play, it becomes a matter of the law. We need you to tell us about the grave, or we're going to have to take you in for further questioning."

"*Mei fraa* left me," Zeb said through gritted teeth. "The grave was for the boy."

Officer Banks put a hand on his gun, the other, reaching for his handcuffs. "You have a boy buried in the grave?"

"*Nee*—no! The grave was for *mei* son's benefit, so he wouldn't know his *mamm* left him! I had a funeral for her so he wouldn't know she left us."

"Why go to all that trouble? Didn't you think about what it would do to your son if she was to come back? Your son might have wanted to see her again."

"I've forbidden her to see him."

"But you just told us she was here with you, and you wanted her to come back. Doesn't your son know she's here?"

Zeb would not face them. "*Nee,* he does not live here, and he does not know I still know her as *mei fraa.* But she ran off again, so you see, it was *gut* that I didn't tell him, or his heart would be breaking the same as mine is now."

The officer eased up a little. "I'm going to need you to show me the grave, Mr. Yoder."

Zeb jumped up into his buggy and picked up the reins. "Unless you are detaining me for something, you can go out there yourself," he said pointing in the direction of the grave. "I have business to take care of in town."

"One more thing, Mr. Yoder. If we need you to dig up that grave to prove that it's empty, are you willing to do that?"

"My son has forgiven me for my shame, but now he will have another burden from his *vadder* if you open that grave," Zeb said angrily.

"You can do it willingly, or we can get a search warrant," the officer warned him.

Zeb slapped the reins, and set his horse in motion without answering the officer. He knew to agree to such a thing would bring further ridicule and shame on his head, and he wanted no part of it.

Chapter 11

Feeling discouraged, Kyle knew there was something he needed to take care of; something he'd put off for too many years. He felt more than ever it was time to face his past once and for all.

He offered to drop the woman off at a few shops downtown so she could pick up a few things for herself. He felt bad that she didn't have proper clothes to wear. She mentioned she'd like to get some material to make a couple of things, and he offered to pay. He even offered to let her stay in his spare room in his apartment, having felt responsible for her safety. In exchange, she offered to cook for him, and he was happy with that arrangement until she could get on her feet and be out on her own.

He didn't know why, perhaps because he missed his own mother so much, but he just couldn't turn her out into the streets or put her up in a women's shelter—especially if she was Caleb's mother. Surely he would want him to care for her until he returned from Florida.

On the drive into town, Kyle shared with her about Greta, and how she'd agreed to see him even though he was an *Englisher.*

"If she's smart," she said. "Greta will let you court her!"

"Don't the Amish believe that courting is like being engaged?"

"*Jah,* they do in a way."

Kyle chuckled nervously. "So if I'm taking her for a buggy ride, does that mean she expects me to marry her?"

"It's possible," she agreed. "Amish girls take courting very seriously."

"I don't want to hurt her," Kyle said. "I like her a lot. I may even be in love with her, but I never planned on getting married."

"Why not?"

Kyle shrugged as he turned off County Road 17, and onto the parkway. "I didn't really have a good sense of family when I was growing up. It didn't make me want one. I would never want to put a kid through what I went through."

"What do you mean?" she asked.

He shrugged again and sighed. "Well, my dad went to prison when I was only four years old, and I didn't have a great relationship with my mom after I left home at the age of ten. I went and stayed with my Uncle—well, I knew he wasn't really my uncle. I took on my mother's maiden name after my father was killed—at least, I think it was her maiden name—I never really knew if anything she told me was the truth. I think she was trying so hard to manage her own bad decisions, that she didn't make the best ones where I was concerned."

"Do you think your mother loved you?"

He smiled. "I know she loved me. There was never any doubt about that. She loved me more than she loved herself, but she didn't love herself much at all. I felt bad for leaving her, but I just couldn't take care of her. She had a sadness in her I just couldn't help her with. I was too young, and I didn't understand what she was going through. I deeply regret leaving her—now that I'm an adult, I really regret that."

"I'm certain she knew you loved her."

"I pray you're right about that."

Kyle put his blinker on and merged onto the off-ramp for Hartford.

"Why are we going here?" she asked.

"I have a little unfinished business to take care of, and I thought it would be safer for you to shop here—away from Old Man Yoder."

She suppressed a smile. "Why do you call him that?'

"Because he's a mean old man! For the short time I've known him, he's never said a kind word to me. He's harsh with his own son, and I've never seen anything other than a scowl on his face."

"He's a very troubled man. You should have some grace for him."

Kyle shook his head as he pulled in front of the downtown area and parked at the fabric store. "That man did something to hurt you, so why didn't you tell the police what he did?"

"It isn't my place to decide if he is punished for his sins. The Amish ways teach us to forgive the transgressions of others. We are not to judge or condemn."

Kyle put the truck in park and turned to her. "Here you are, ma'am. Curbside service. I'll be back to pick you up in about an hour, and we'll get a cup of hot cocoa and pie at the diner. Go there when you finish, and I'll meet you there."

She opened the door to the truck and turned to Kyle, and smiled. *"Danki."*

"By the way, if you and I are going to be roommates for a while, what should I call you? I still don't know your name. Do you even know it?"

"Ma'am is fine for now."

Kyle smirked. "Have it your way. But sooner or later, you're going to have to trust me!"

She smiled.

"I'll see you in an hour," he said, just before she closed the door.

Chapter 12

Kyle stood outside his old apartment building, looking up at the window his mother used to hang out of when she'd call him inside from playing stickball in the street with the neighbor kids. He closed his eyes and listened to the street noises. They hadn't changed much since he was a kid; sirens that could be heard for miles, kids playing…he was back home in his element.

"Kyle Albee!" a familiar voice yelled from up above. "What are you doing down there in the snow? Get up here and give me some sugar!"

He smiled, as he looked up at his old landlady, who was hanging out of the third-floor window and frantically unpinning pink, foam curlers from her hair.

"I'll be right up, Mrs. Haverty."

She pushed down on the window and shivered, wrapping the same terrycloth robe around her that should have been tossed in the rag pile years ago. He chuckled to himself, thinking nothing had really changed—except for him.

He stomped the slush off his boots and walked up three flights to visit a woman who was so much a part of his childhood. Before he had a chance to knock, the door swung open and he was greeted with a pair of chubby arms that pulled him into a squishy hug there was no way out of except to wait for it to end.

"Oh, it's so good to see you," the older woman cried. "I thought I'd never see my little Kyle again."

She rocked him back and forth as she cried and laughed at the same time. She'd always been the emotional type, but she was a good woman. She'd always get after him when he needed to be gotten after, and she looked out for his mom in her own way—mostly by making sure he took care of her.

"*Take care of your momma,*" she would reprimand him. "*She took care of you when you were a baby, and now it's your turn to care for her.*"

He'd never forgotten the look of shame she'd given him when he left, but apparently, all was forgiven now, as her hug would suggest.

She pulled him away from her and swatted him in the arm.

Alright, perhaps not!

"Why haven't you come to visit sooner?" she said, tears streaming down her ample cheeks. "I'm an old woman, and I'm not going to be around forever, you know!"

"I'm sorry, Mrs. Haverty. I guess I just needed to sort some things out."

She pushed him into her apartment, which covered the entire third floor of the building she and her husband owned.

"And have you sorted them out, or have you come to me for answers?" she asked, ushering him into the kitchen.

He sat down in the chair she pointed to, and she immediately had a glass of milk and a plate of cookies in front of him—just like when he was younger and he would go up there to pay the rent.

"A little of both," he admitted, stuffing a cookie into his mouth and chasing it with a gulp of milk.

"Would you like the box of her things I have up in the attic? It isn't much. I donated most of it, but I kept a few things that were too curious to get rid of—just in case you had questions later about her, mind you."

"What sort of things?"

"Well, for one thing, the Amish clothes she wore when she first arrived on my doorstep."

Kyle swallowed down hard a chunk of cookie, coughing to keep from choking on it. "Amish clothes? Are you sure? Why would my mother be wearing Amish clothes?"

Mrs. Haverty shrugged. "I didn't ask, and she never told. From the time she moved in until the time of her death, I never saw the clothes again, so I'd forgotten all about them."

Kyle's eyes grew wide. "What are you talking about?"

"When I found her—when she died—she was wearing Amish clothes then, too, but it was a different dress than what she'd worn when she first came here. She was just a young girl then—pregnant with you."

"What about my father?"

She stood from her chair and went to the refrigerator and pulled the carton of milk out and refilled Kyle's glass automatically.

"You mean the one that went to jail? What was his name again?"

"Bruce—Albee."

"Oh yes, Bruce. They got married just a few days before you arrived into this world, but you sure were the apple of his eye."

"He didn't marry her *before* she got pregnant for me?"

"No, but I don't know the whole story about that. I would hear them arguing sometimes. I could hear them all the way up here from the ground floor. I suppose that's why she didn't marry him at first. He never wore Amish clothes, but he had Amish friends. They used to come over, and then one day stopped—about the same time he went to prison. But then one Amish man started coming around again to see your mother. About a week before I found your mother when she'd overdosed from the pills, the man came to see her and brought an Amish woman with him. After that, I couldn't get your mother to open the door. She stayed in the apartment and didn't come out. One day, I decided to knock to see if she needed anything when I went to the market, and I heard a crash and glass breaking. I used my master key to open the door, and she was lying on the floor in the Amish clothes. She'd fallen on that glass table she had in the living room, and her face was cut badly. I called an ambulance, but she didn't make it."

Kyle ran a hand through his thick hair. Hearing about her death put a lump in his throat, and a heaviness in his heart.

He'd forgotten about the slash in her face. They'd tried to cover it up when they'd made her up for the funeral, but she just didn't look very much like herself. He'd used his pocket knife to steal a lock of her hair at the funeral home when the director's back was turned. It was the only thing he had left of her.

"That isn't the strangest thing I found in your apartment when I was cleaning out her things."

Kyle stood up, wishing he hadn't eaten so many cookies because they were now souring in his stomach. "What else could be stranger than that?"

"The strong-box at the back of her closet with the key stuck in the lock. It had a lot of money in it and a note to you! I've been waiting for you to come back and claim it."

Kyle shook the anxiety from his head. "How much money?"

The woman's eyes grew wide and dramatic. "Twenty-five-thousand dollars!"

"How did she get her hands on that kind of money? We were poor!"

Kyle fell to his knees, his heart breaking. "The robbery!" he whispered.

Chapter 13

"Start from the beginning," Kyle said. "I want to know how you know Old Man Yoder!"

He paced the floor of his townhouse apartment, while the old woman sat on the floor with her back against the sofa, cutting navy blue material for a dress.

"I suppose it all started when we were young," she said, resting the fabric on her lap, and looking off in the distance as if reflecting another time. "I was very much in love with Zeb Yoder. He was a fine young man and very handsome—back then. There was a time when he smiled all the time, and I was in love with him. But I wasn't his first choice. My younger sister, Rose, was his first choice. I was very envious of her at the time. I was older than she was, and I felt she was too young for him. While we were on our *rumspringa*, I decided I would have Zeb with wild abandon. I thought I could take his heart from my sister, but all I did was end up pregnant. I knew he didn't want to marry me, and so I ran away and I left the community."

"And yet he now calls you his wife?" Kyle asked angrily.

"I replaced her, because she rejected him, but I'll tell you about that in a minute. But at the time, he married Rose. I never got over him. He was my first love. I still continued to see him behind my sister's back and I'm ashamed of that, and when she found out, she left him."

"That would make you Caleb's aunt!"

She nodded, biting her bottom lip.

"So that's why there's a grave out back of the Yoder's property," he asked.

"*Jah*," she answered.

Kyle held his head. "If you ask me, I think you didn't tell the police what you know because you're afraid of the old man—not that I blame you. He's a pretty disturbed man. Why did you go back with him?"

"With Rose out of the picture, I thought I'd won, but instead, Zeb made me pay for leaving him the first time. At first, things were *gut* between us, and I thought we could be happy together. But as time went by, I realized he was keeping me hidden like a dirty secret. He became angry one day when Caleb saw me across the pond. Caleb thought I was his mother—back from the dead! He became so irate, in fact, that he decided he would tie me up and put me in the cellar in the barn. I was never allowed outside again."

"He tied you up?" Kyle asked.

"Jah," she said. "But that wasn't the worst of it."

"How could it get worse than that?"

She lowered her head averting his gaze, feelings of shame rising up from her spirit.

"That first night he tied me up, was the night Bruce Albee was killed in the barn."

Kyle's eyes widened, his attention gripping her every word. "So then you saw Amelia shoot him?"

"*Jah*, I saw him get shot," she said, tears in her eyes. "But I saw Zeb shoot him and kill him."

Kyle couldn't breathe. He paced the floor in front of her, wringing his sweaty hands. "What are you talking about?" he asked. "Amelia confessed to the shooting. She shot him with the Derringer she found in the barn. She said she pulled the trigger by accident, but the gun went off, and the bullet went straight through his heart."

She set aside her sewing, too agitated to concentrate on it.

"*Nee*," she said, correcting him. "It was the bullet from Zeb's gun that killed him. The shot from the gun in Amelia's hand went up above his head and missed him completely." She demonstrated by raising her arms and pivoting them backward really fast to show that her arms jerked upward when Bruce lurched toward her.

Kyle thought about the bullet he'd found lodged in the crossbeam in the barn, thinking it was all starting to make sense.

"I saw the whole thing," she continued. "The two of them shot the guns almost at the same time, and it was so close, that it sounded almost like one shot, with a bit of an echo. I knew the truth, but only because I saw it with my own eyes."

Kyle raked a shaky hand through his hair, fighting the bile that was threatening to come up.

"Because of this, Zeb left me in the cellar for nearly a week—that time."

"I wish you would tell the police all of this. I know you're afraid. I am too, but he needs help. Help we can't give him."

"I only want to break free from him."

"But he belongs in Jail!" Kyle insisted.

"Nee, I already told you, it's not my place to pass judgement. I must forgive him. It is my Amish wisdom that gives me peace to forgive. Any man can lose his way and go apart from *Gott*—even an Amish man."

"But this is different," Kyle argued. "He killed a man. He killed my father!"

"It is not for you or me to judge. *Gott* will do that in *His* timing, not ours."

Kyle was seething with anger. Bruce's death was more than eight years ago, but the pain was rising in him as fresh as it was when he was just a young boy and had lost both his parents in the span of a few days. He hadn't even had a chance to see his father after he'd gotten out of prison. He'd forgiven Amelia for shooting him, but if she didn't shoot him, he'd have to forgive the offense all over again.

"Did you even know Bruce Albee?"

She lowered her head in shame. "Yes, I knew him because I knew about the robbery. I didn't play a part, other than keeping quiet about it, but I was there the night Zeb shot him!"

"All this time, Amelia thought she'd shot him with the gun she found in Old Man Yoder's barn! The guilt almost ruined her life."

"I'm sorry for her, but that's not how it happened. Zeb was there that night, tying me up in the barn when Bruce walked in after Amelia. Zeb shot him to get revenge."

"Revenge for what?"

"Mostly because of the money, but there were other reasons too."

"There isn't ever any good reason for that kind of revenge," Kyle said.

The woman sighed, tears pooling in her eyes. "I'm afraid I feel drained. I can't talk about this too much without it causing me anxiety."

Kyle looked at her, feeling like a heel when he saw how much she was shaking.

"We can talk more about this later," he offered.

She looked at him, her eyes softened. "Perhaps the journal will shed some light on it."

He shook his head and wagged his finger at her. "Oh, no! You're not going to talk me into breaking into Old Man Yoder's house and getting you that journal."

Chapter 14

Kyle's heart raced and his sweaty hands shook as
he went to the door and turned the knob, opening
the kitchen door at Old Man Yoder's house. He
didn't dare second-guess himself, for fear he
would have too much time to talk himself out of
it. He couldn't believe she'd managed to convince
him to follow along with such a crazy scheme, but
if it meant proving the old man's guilt in some
way, he would do it for the sake of putting this
nightmare to rest once and for all.

He'd promised the old woman he would do this
one last favor, but only after she promised him a
full explanation, claiming she owed him that

much. Admittedly, he agreed with her on that account. But she'd all-but-threatened to go fetch the journal herself if he didn't go after it, and so he'd reluctantly allowed her to talk him into going in her stead.

Kyle had watched from the window of Caleb's house until he'd seen the old man drive off in his buggy, but that didn't mean he'd stay away. Remembering the last encounter with the old man when he'd gotten locked in the cellar made him shiver. But the possible violence he'd experienced in Caleb's *dawdi haus* a couple of nights ago was enough to set his teeth on edge.

Admittedly, he was nervous about leaving the woman in a home so close to the Yoder farm, but he figured having her where he could see potential danger was better than having her across town.

As he walked through the old man's house, he followed the path the woman had instructed him to take, and he wondered if he would serve time for breaking and entering, even though the door was unlocked. He supposed since he hadn't gotten an invitation, the law might consider it breaking in regardless of the door being unlocked. Those were all technicalities he couldn't afford to think about right now, especially since he'd made the decision to go ahead with the old woman's plan. She had assured him that she had rights to the home, and he assumed that was because she was living there for the past several years. With her permission to enter the home, he could hardly think he'd be held accountable for breaking and entering.

So why did he get the feeling she was leaving out a vital piece of the puzzle—perhaps purposefully, in order to get him to do her bidding? He didn't exactly feel manipulated, but he'd been talked into a caper he thought certain was a bad idea.

He cringed from every little creek in the stairs. Though he knew no one was home, it didn't stop him from trying to be quiet. His only goal was to retrieve the woman's journal she claimed was tucked away behind a loose brick in the fireplace up in the attic. To her, it was her entire life. To him, it would answer the myriad of questions that plagued him about the Yoder family.

Once he entered the attic, he immediately suppressed a sneeze. A thick layer of dust coated everything that didn't have a sheet draped over it. Even the floor was dusty, and it didn't take him long to see his footprints from the sunbeam that sprayed light across the floor, illuminating the undisturbed room now littered with his tracks. Regardless of whether he made it out of this predicament safely, his footprints would surely tell on him, and the old man would come looking for him; there was no doubt in his mind about that.

Since there was nothing to do now but follow through with the plan, Kyle forced himself to move toward the back of the room where he could see the red bricks of the chimney. He was so close; he could taste his freedom from this nightmare.

When he reached the chimney, he located the area the woman had instructed him and began to feel around for loose bricks. When he found the one in the back that jiggled, he craned his neck around to see between the bricks and the wall. Pulling the set of bricks from their place, he blindly pushed his hand into the opening, trying not to think of the spiders or mice that could be inhabiting the space. Thankfully, his fingers made contact with a thick book with a soft leather cover, and he pulled it free. Mortar dust covered it, so he tipped it and blew it off. Seeing the cover, he realized the book was not a journal, but a record-keeping book.

Was there another book in there?

He reached his hand into the space and found nothing. Curious, he opened the book to be sure he had what she'd asked for. He wasn't about to attempt this caper again.

Moving into the sunlight from the window, he could see there was writing in the book instead of figures that would measure book-keeping. He flipped through several more pages to be sure, when his gaze fell on his father's name within the pages. He read the sentence, which spurred him to read further, until he realized he was reading the passage that explained the events of his shooting that night. There it was, written in ink, the record of his father's murder—at the hands of Zeb Yoder.

Anger rose up in him as he stuffed the book in the waist of his jeans behind his jacket. If he should run into the old man, the last thing he wanted was for him to catch him with the evidence he needed to put the man in jail where he belonged.

Quickly replacing the bricks with shaky hands, Kyle wanted only to leave the man's house and take the book directly to the police instead of the old woman. He didn't intend to betray her, but he wanted justice for his father's death, and if that meant forcing her to answer for the words she'd written in the *journal,* then that's what he would do.

Tiptoeing back to the door, Kyle listened for a moment to be sure he wouldn't be met with any surprises on the other side. Turning the handle slowly, he opened the door, aware of every creak that echoed so dramatically, it caused him to cringe.

Once outside the door, he closed it behind him and let out the breath he'd been holding in.

"That's far enough," Zeb's gruff voice echoed from the end of the hall behind him.

Kyle could feel his heart beating double-time, the sound of the man's heavy foot-falls muffled only by the blood rushing to his head from his over-active heart.

He turned slowly, and the old man stopped just short of him. Shotgun in hand, Zeb's gaze narrowed on Kyle, the furrow in his brow cinched and unyielding.

"You're trespassing!"

Kyle had no good explanation other than the truth, which he thought might appease the man. "I was looking for something for Caleb's aunt. She said she left some of her things in your attic, and she sent me to fetch them."

Zeb chuckled madly. "Caleb's *aenti?* Is that who she told you she was?"

Kyle nodded, not understanding the way he'd asked the question. As if she was not who she claimed to be. Had the woman lied to him? No! She didn't seem capable of such a thing. But yet, here he was, breaking into a man's house at her request, and he really didn't know who she was.

"I told you boy, if you didn't bring her back here, you'd be replacing her!" he said, aiming the shotgun at him.

"I'm not going to hand her over to you so you can keep her here like she's your property. She's not going to be your prisoner anymore!"

Kyle's rasping breaths increased with anger. "Are you going to shoot me like you did my father? Amelia didn't shoot him—you did! You killed my father!"

"Your father?" the old man asked, throwing his head back and laughing madly. "I didn't kill your father—I *am* your father!"

His words shook Kyle to his very core.

"It isn't true!" he said, backing away from him.

"It's true, didn't your *mother* tell you?"

"Bruce is my father, and you killed him!"

"Turn around and walk out to the barn. I warned you boy. I told you if you didn't bring her back you would take her place. Move it!" he said, keeping the shotgun trained on him.

Kyle couldn't move. His mind was numb thinking about this man being his father. He refused to believe it.

"I said, turn around, or I'll shoot!" the man growled.

He turned, but only slightly, giving himself enough room to see any fast movements. "Is that thing even loaded?" he asked lightly, remembering his encounter with Amelia's mom.

He pumped the barrel, engaging the bullets in the chamber of the gun; that sound unmistakable.

"You care to find out?"

Kyle shook his head, his eyes bulging.

He was trapped, and he would be hard-pressed to get away unless he used his wit. He feared if he fought the old man, he'd get knocked out again. Cooperation was his only chance of survival. Perhaps keeping him talking would make a difference.

"If I'm really your son like you say," Kyle said with a shaky voice. "Why would you shoot me?"

"You betrayed me!" he said, marching Kyle out of the house and through the field toward the barn. "Just like my dear Rose did."

"I haven't betrayed you," Kyle tried reasoning with him.

Feeling the barrel of the gun press between his shoulder blades, Kyle struggled to think of a way out. The man had obviously lost his mind, and was capable of anything. But with a gun to his back, he was powerless. It would seem that since he was planning on holding him in the old woman's stead, perhaps he would ride this out, and find a way to escape after the man cooled down. Besides, she knew he was there, and if he didn't return, he'd instructed her to call the police. Could he count on her for that? He supposed he'd have to; he had no other choice.

Once inside the dark barn, the old man ordered him to light the lantern he'd lit once before. Then he ordered him to open the cellar door and go down inside.

"Don't do this!" Kyle begged. "If I'm really your son, how can you do this to your own flesh and blood?"

"Your mother betrayed me!" he said. "She kept you from me and made another man your father."

"I had no idea," he said.

"Everyone betrays me, and I can't let you get away with it! Rose didn't get away with it. She wouldn't listen to reason. I *had* to poison her with the pills," he rambled on.

Fear consumed Kyle, his blood pumping his heart to a speed that made him gasp for air. The pressure rose in his head, making him dizzy with terror. He steadied himself against the pole the lantern hung from.

He killed his wife. He's going to kill me, and the woman too when he catches her.

Rage filled Kyle with adrenalin. "You're not my father; I had a father and you killed him!"

"If you don't believe me," he said calmly. "You can ask your *mother*!"

Kyle felt the twinge of fear pour through him at the realization of his statement.

The old woman was his mother, and they would both die at the hands of this bitter and sick man if he didn't do something to stop him.

Grasping the lantern with his fingers, Kyle lifted it swiftly, without a second thought, and flung it against the floor, spilling out the oil.

Startled by the sparks that quickly ignited to flames, spreading over the fresh layer of straw on the floor, Zeb rushed at Kyle, tackling him to the ground. As his head hit the wood floor, his eyes closed, and his world went black.

Chapter 15

Selma peeked out the kitchen window nervously when a car pulled into the driveway of Caleb's house. She watched a young couple exit a taxicab, and realized she recognized him as her nephew.

She smoothed Kyle's baggy shirt and pants over her tiny frame, realizing it didn't matter what she looked like; she was going to have to give an explanation to the nephew she never really knew, and he'd likely be more worried about having a person in his house he didn't know than what she looked like. She had to admit, though, she felt like she looked homeless, which in a way, she was.

Caleb sniffed the air when he exited the cab. He smelled smoke, and it was the wrong season to be burning leaves. He promptly handed the driver the money and retrieved his luggage.

"Do you smell that?" Amelia asked.

He nodded. "Let's get you inside, and then I'll check it out. I'm sure it's nothing."

Before he could reach the door, Selma came running from the house and approached the couple out of breath.

"Your father's barn is on fire, and I think Kyle is over there. He's in trouble. I don't have time to explain, but you need to help him!" she said.

"Who are you?" Caleb asked.

"I'm Kyle's mother! Please help him!"

"Kyle's mother? I thought you were dead!"

"I was—sort of, but he rescued me. It's a long story, and I don't have time to go into it right now. I think he's in danger and I need you to help him!"

Caleb looked at her familiar face and the realization hit him all at once. "You stay here," he said to his wife and the woman claiming to be Kyle's mother. "I'll go see what's going on."

He took off running through the field toward the burning barn, his thoughts reeling. How could that woman be Kyle's mother? Was she the same woman he'd seen on too many occasions wandering his own property as a child?

He ran faster, seeing the flames licking the top of the barn roof, smoke billowing out from it. When he approached, he nearly ran into the electric fence that stood between him and the burning barn.

When and why had his dad put that up?

Admittedly, he hadn't gone near the barn since Amelia got hurt when she was caught in the barbed wire he had put up. Caleb hadn't known about that either. But electric fence? How was he going to get to the barn—especially if Kyle was in there like the woman claimed? And what did his father have to do with Kyle being in danger?

He didn't have time to run all the way up to the main house to get in through the yard. Looking around for a way in, he realized the only way in would be to climb the tree that hung over the fence.

When he jumped to the drifted snow under the tree branch, it wasn't as soft as he'd hoped it would be, and his feet throbbed from the high jump. He hobbled over toward the barn, calling out to Kyle.

From inside the barn, Kyle could hear someone calling his name. He coughed and drew in a breath, his lungs and throat burning from the smoke. Crawling toward the voice, he could see the barn door opening.

It was Caleb.

He ducked his head against the billowing smoke and rushed to Kyle's side, grabbing his shirt and pulling him toward the door.

Once they were out in the yard, Caleb dropped him in the snow, and collapsed next to him. They coughed and he patted Kyle on the back.

"How many times am I going to have to pull you from burning buildings?"

Kyle coughed and wiped soot from his face. "I'm praying this will be the last time!"

"What happened," Caleb asked. "Why were you in there?"

Kyle struggled to his feet, still feeling a little disoriented.

"Your dad! It's my fault. I started the fire, and your dad's still in there!"

He ran toward the barn and Caleb followed him in, the two of them pulling their coats over their faces to shield from the smoke. They stayed together, keeping low.

Kyle went toward the middle of the barn where he'd smashed the lantern, and found him lying on the floor. They both grabbed him, but he fought them.

"Leave me in here," he growled. "I need to burn for my sins."

"I'm not leaving you in here, no matter what you've done!" Kyle yelled at him.

Dragging him against his will, the two of them struggled, while the fire crackled and the roof creaked.

"We need to get out of here before the roof collapses!" Caleb hollered above the roaring of the fire.

Grabbing a support beam, Zeb tried to fight the two of them, until Caleb peeled his fingers from the pole, while Kyle grabbed his legs.

"Let—me—die!" he yelled between coughs, still struggling and fighting the two who were trying to rescue him.

Finally, they got him out of the barn and onto the snowy ground several feet away. As they collapsed in the snow beside their father, they looked up and watched the barn roof start to give-way. They both jumped up fast and pulled the old man further away, while he yelled at them.

"Leave me alone," he said, yanking his arms free. "You should have left me in there to die!"

Off in the distance, the sound of approaching fire trucks brought relief to Caleb.

He turned to his father. "Why do you want to die?"

He sat there silent.

"Tell him!" Kyle said angrily. "Tell him how you shot Bruce Albee and blamed it on Amelia! And how you poisoned his mother, and locked mine away for the last several years. Tell him that you're *my* father too!"

The old man remained silent, his eyes cast down.

Caleb looked at Kyle, who was breathing hard, anger clenching his jaw.

He turned to his father, tears welling up in his eyes. "Is this true?"

The old man just sat there, staring at the snow, but he wouldn't say a word.

Chapter 16

Caleb paced the floor of the hospital's emergency room waiting area, waiting to hear from the doctor who was examining his father.

Amelia stood and met him, interrupting his path.

"Come sit," she urged him. "All this pacing isn't going to make the doctors hurry, but you're going to wear yourself out."

He pulled her into his arms and leaned down to kiss her cheek. "In all this excitement," he whispered to her. "I forgot to tell you something."

She looked at him, worry in her eyes. "What else is there? Is there more to this story than Kyle being your brother?"

He sighed. "My father is the one that shot Bruce Albee. Your bullet was stuck in the rafters of the barn. Kyle told me he has pictures of it. My father confessed it to Kyle, Selma saw him shoot Bruce that night. She said your bullet shot up into the rafters over Bruce's head."

Amelia buried her face in his chest and began to weep quietly. "All this time, I've tormented myself over this. I'm relieved my bullet is not the one that killed that man, but I'm sorry it was your father who did it."

He hugged her tightly. "Me too!"

Kyle leaned in to talk quietly with his mom. "I think we still have a lot to talk about," he said to her. "But I need to talk to my brother about a few things too. Right now, he's too concerned with the old man, but I'm going to have to tell him about his mom. But first, I need you to tell me how she ended up in *your* grave."

Tears filled her eyes. "I never meant to hurt my sister—or you for that matter. I'm ashamed that I was still seeing Zeb even while he was married to my sister, Rose. I just never got over him. When she found out, she threatened to go to the Bishop with his indiscretion, and then told him she was going to leave him. He brought her to my apartment and told her she could stay there, and asked me to come back with him. I thought I was going to live in the house with him, and could eventually bring you back there with me."

"So the two of you switched places, and I never knew because I just didn't come home. I was having too much fun with my cousins."

"I would never have left her there if I'd known Zeb would go back and poison her. He confessed to me that he gave her tea with the sleeping pills in it. I didn't know whether or not what he said was true, but I didn't want to take the chance of it happening to me. After all, I depended on him to feed me all those years. As long as I didn't fight him, I wasn't locked up. So when I found out my sister was buried as *me,* I was trying to escape. We'd had an argument that day, and he showed me the obituary from Caleb's mother, but they named *me* as the deceased. That's when I tried to get away from him, but he locked me in the cellar, and I'd been there for about a week before I hit him over the head and escaped—the night you found me. When I threatened to expose him for his lies and abuse, he laughed and told me no one would believe a dead woman; that they would think I was crazy. After all, there was a grave with my name on it, and you'd had a funeral for me. To the world, I was a dead woman. I couldn't fight that."

Kyle pulled her hand into his and squeezed it. "I'm glad I found you."

"I am too," she said. "I'm sorry I wasn't there for you as much as I should have been. I know it's no excuse, but I suffered a lot of anxiety after leaving the community, and I went to doctors that gave me medicine that made things worse, so I didn't take them. I was sad all the time without my parents and the community. I was lost, and didn't know how to take care of a child on my own. Bruce was good to you, I don't know if you remember him, but when his friends came to him about the robbery, he was too quick to take the easy way out. Prison obviously turned him bitter, Zeb had blamed the entire thing on him, and witnessed against him as revenge for marrying me, and then eventually killed him for the same reason."

"If you weren't his first choice, and he didn't marry you, why did he care that you married Bruce?"

She sighed, fidgeting with the sleeve of the coat Amelia had given her to wear. "I don't know, other than he took it personally when I rejected him—after he'd rejected me! He is a very possessive and territorial man, but he's also very dangerous—to himself, and those he claims to love."

"What about the money? Is that from the robbery?"

She nodded. "We need to turn that money in. I'd wanted you to have it, but turning it in is the right thing to do."

"I was afraid you'd say that," he said with a chuckle.

The doctors finally returned to the waiting room to talk to them, and the two brothers sat together to support each other.

"Your father suffered from mild smoke inhalation, but he didn't have a stroke like we thought when you first brought him in," the doctor explained. "We've sent him upstairs to be evaluated, as it seems he may have suffered some trauma, and he's in a catatonic state. He hasn't spoken or responded even once since he's been here. He's in the psychiatric ward on the third floor. I think they'll hold him there twenty-four hours, unless a family member admits him for therapy, but we might also suggest putting him in a nursing home."

The two of them sat there, unable to make a decision, and so the doctor excused himself, and referred them to the third floor nursing station.

"What should we do with him?" Kyle asked after the doctor left them. "We need to decide if we should turn him in."

"He's committed crimes," Caleb said. "I understand this, but it is not our place to judge. I think he needs help, but I believe he needs prayer more than anything."

He patted Kyle on the back. "I have to say, I still can't get over the fact you're my brother!"

Kyle smirked at him and punched him playfully. "Half-brother! But I'm glad too. It's nice to have a family."

Caleb smiled. "I have an *aenti* and a new brother. Hey, do you realize this makes you Amish, Kyle?"

He sat next to his mom and leaned his head on her shoulder. "I hadn't even thought about that. I guess that means I can marry Greta!"

Selma nudged at her son. "I thought you said you were never getting married."

"That was before I found out I had a family. Besides, I think I'm in love with her. I know we only had one date, but it was a wonderful date, and I think I'm going to ask her to court."

"I'll make you a proper Amish shirt and trousers to wear so you can court her proper-like!" his mother said.

"But how can I court her *proper-like* if I don't have a proper Amish name? I know Jack Sinclair was not your brother, who was he?"

"He was a *gut* friend of Bruce's, and his *fraa*, Miriam, was my very best friend growing up. She and I both ran from the community when we became pregnant. It was something we had in common, and we leaned on each other. You and her oldest, Seth, were like cousins. How could I tell you anything different? I'm sorry you took on their name because you felt so lost."

"I know Zeb is my *father*, but I have no desire to carry on his name. I feel like a man without a country!"

"You can always take my *real* maiden name. It was Graber."

"Graber; I like that. Now that's a proper Amish name!"

Selma giggled and kissed her grown-up, baby boy on his cheek.

He leaned back and took in the reality of having a brother, but getting his mom back was almost surreal.

"Boy, won't Greta be surprised when she finds out I'm Amish!"

THE END

Please turn the page to read a sneak peek FIRST CHAPTER of the NEXT book in this series!

SNEAK PEEK

BOOK 3

Chapter 1

"He asked to see the Bishop," Caleb told Kyle.

"Do you trust him?"

"I think we have no choice. I believe he wants to confess to the Bishop before he turns himself in. He told me he knows he needs to pay for the crimes he committed."

"Do you think it's wise to take him back home? I'm not sure any of us are safe," Kyle asked nervously.

"I know he's done wrong, and he agrees he needs to turn himself in, but he's our father, and I think we should let him speak to the Bishop first."

"I suppose you're right," Kyle agreed. "But do you really think he should be around my mom and Amelia?"

"They're safe and sound at your house with the doors locked, and we removed all his guns from his house. Besides, it's only for an hour while he meets with the Bishop."

They waited outside the same locked room Kyle's mom was in only two days before, while the nurse slid her card in the lock to release him.

Zeb Yoder took his time in meeting them in the hallway, not seeming interested in leaving.

"We have a search warrant to search the premises and we brought a crew to dig up the grave your father buried some years ago. He's claimed it's empty, but there are laws against this sort of thing, whether the casket is empty or not."

Kyle and Caleb looked at the five-man crew wearing reflective vests and toting shovels, who stood behind the two police officers.

"We're going to need your father to go with us out to the grave site."

"He's in the middle of a confession with our Bishop right now, can you wait a few minutes?"

"I'm afraid we're on a schedule," the officer said. "The city is paying these men to be here, and the city won't pay for your father to finish his visit."

"I'll get him," Caleb said.

When he returned with his father, the Bishop agreed to go with him for support, and Caleb thought it was more out of curiosity than anything else. Surely the rest of the community would hear about all of this before it even hit the newspapers.

One of the officers asked Zeb to step outside on the porch. "Are you Zebedee Yoder?"

He nodded. "*Jah.*"

The officer pulled out a pair of handcuffs and proceeded to read him his rights.

"What are you doing?" Kyle asked.

The officer ignored Kyle until he was finished. "Do you understand these rights?"

Zeb nodded again.

"Your father is under arrest for improper burial, and violating the city and county ordinances regarding placement of graves."

Knowing Zeb had committed far worse crimes than this, Kyle still wanted to make sure the man was being charged fairly. "But the grave is empty!"

"That doesn't matter!" the officer said. "There are codes and regulations regarding burials of anything other than house-pets, and your father broke the law."

"But he didn't bury anything other than a casket!" Kyle continued to argue.

"Let's go dig up the casket so we can be sure it's empty," the officer said.

After all that had happened, Kyle had to admit he was just as curious to see if it was empty.

"Is that *really* against the law?" Caleb asked his brother.

Kyle shrugged, as they followed the officers out to the site. "I've heard of some strange laws on the books, so who knows. But I'm thinking they should have brought a back-hoe to dig it up. They're going to have fun cutting through the frozen ground with those shovels."

When they reached the site, one of the men removed the grave marker, a nice cross Caleb had carved for his mother, and tossed it to the ground. Upset by this, he went over and retrieved it. After his father went to confess, he planned on having a proper burial for his mother, and that cross would serve as a grave marker wherever they put her.

The men began to dig, and everyone else stood by and watched. They made light work digging up the shallow grave, brushing it off and pulling it from the earth.

"It's heavy," one of them said, turning to Zeb. "I thought you said this casket was empty."

"It is. I only buried it for my son's sake, so he wouldn't know his mother had chosen to leave him."

Caleb cringed. More lies. *Aenti* Selma had told him that Zeb had forbidden her to see her son again. Did his father even know the truth anymore?

"Open it up!" the officer ordered the men.

Two of them used their shovels to pry open the casket. When they flipped open the lid, they all cringed and backed away, holding their hands over their faces and groaning, but Kyle and Caleb were not close enough to see what the problem was.

As the wind shifted, the stench of death consumed them.

All eyes peered in to see the deceased, fully clad in an Amish dress and *kapp*.

***

This is the end of the Sneak Peak. I hope you enjoyed it. Be looking for BOOK THREE in this series. Coming soon!

You might also enjoy…

Made in the USA
San Bernardino, CA
08 November 2016